GREAT AUNT PEPPER

GREAT AUNT PEPPER

Roz Southey

SHORTLIST

This Large Print edition published
2012 by AudioGO Ltd
by arrangement with
the Juliet Burton Literary Agency

ISBN 978 1 4713 1344 8

British Library Cataloguing in Publication Data available

Printed and bound in Great Britain by
MPG Books Group Limited

1

It was one of those small square photographs, taken on a box Brownie. Black and white. It showed a seaside resort, with holidaymakers cavorting in the sea, but the elderly woman in the foreground wasn't dressed for a sunny beach—she wore a thick black coat, buttoned up, and a black hat that sat squarely and unflatteringly on her head. Judging by the bathing costumes, the picture had been taken in the early 1960s, but the woman looked as if she'd stepped straight out of the 1940s.

I turned the picture over. Two words were scrawled on the back in my father's writing: *Aunt Pepper.* Which presumably made her my great aunt. I'd never heard of her.

The kitchen door burst open; Liam stared open-mouthed at all the old photographs scattered across the floor. 'Aunt Madge! Whatever are you doing?'

He was wearing a yellow tee shirt with at least three holes, and jeans with deliberate rips around the knees. A year and a half ago, when my nephew Liam first came to stay with me, he'd been dressed in sedate jumpers and slacks, too lacking in self-confidence to risk anything more trendy. Amazing what university can do for you.

'You can't have gone out dressed like that, surely!'

He sighed. 'Aunt Madge! You're beginning to sound like mum!'

Heaven forbid. I grabbed one of the kitchen chairs and hauled myself upright. 'Besides, you're not old enough to say boring things like that,' Liam said severely, looking at me from under his fringe. Ridiculous: he was twenty one, just finishing his course and he looked about twelve. And yes, I was envious.

'I'm retired,' I reminded him. 'As

of today.' Monday: and the thought of all the things I could have been doing came back to me. Chatting in the photocopier room, nipping into the secretaries' room to see if Jenny had had her baby yet, finishing off that contract for the Music Festival. I'd done the publicity for that contract for five years now, and the thought of it going ahead without me . . . But it had been my own choice to take early retirement at the age of 54, knowing that if I did, someone younger might not have to lose their job. Besides, they'd promised to keep in touch.

I just hadn't anticipated feeling so . . . directionless.

I pulled myself together. 'I'm going to do all the things I've been planning to do for years. And the first thing is researching our family history.'

Liam picked his way through the photographs to the kettle, checked the water level and plugged it in.

'Who's that?' He waved at the photo I held.

'Great Aunt Pepper.'

He burst into giggles. One of the reasons I've enjoyed having Liam living with me the last couple of years is his sense of humour. 'No one's called Pepper! What did she do?'

'I haven't a clue. I never knew she existed until a moment ago.'

'Okay!' he said. 'Where do we start? I need something to take my mind off whether I've got a degree or not.'

'Silly,' I said fondly. 'Of course you've got a degree.'

He nodded glumly. 'But will it be good enough?' He stirred water into the mugs, more furiously than was strictly necessary. 'I mean, there aren't many jobs out there, are there?' He tiptoed through the photographs to hand me one of the mugs. 'I'm not even sure I *want* a job. I mean, I want the money, obviously, but the thought of spending all my life in an office ...'

'Then go and work on a farm,' I suggested. Which sent us both into giggles, remembering the one and only time his mother—my sister Judith—had taken Liam out into the country, and the state they'd both come back in. If there was mud, Liam had always been able to find it.

Odd that he was starting out in life, just as I was finishing up in it. No, not in life—in *employment*. There was a difference.

'Do you seriously want to help with the family history?'

He nodded. 'Sounds fun. What do we do first?'

I stared at the photograph again. Great Aunt Pepper had been remarkably stern. Maybe she'd just been concentrating on staying still for the camera. 'Let's start with this lady. They say you should always question older members of the family to get their stories. Let's do that.'

Liam groaned.

'Having second thoughts?'

He swallowed tea in a hurry. 'I'll just go and put something tidier on.'

*   *   *

My father was one of four children: three brothers and a sister. My aunt Jane died about three years ago, of breast cancer, and my father followed not long after, of a heart attack. That left Uncles George and Philip, neither of whom I'd ever particularly got on with.

'I haven't seen George since your mother's birthday.' Both uncles had put in an appearance at Judith's party though I hadn't exchanged more than a *would you like another drink?* with either of them. Judith had always been their favourite; she'd even spent holidays with them as a child, which I'd never been invited to do.

I swallowed the faint traces of old resentments, concentrated on my driving. The houses on Uncle George's estate were semi-detached, with impeccable front lawns, and borders of yellow begonias and scarlet geraniums. Each had their own garage with a white door, and a large car on the hard-standing in front. Number 84 was on a corner, with a tall privet hedge immaculately trimmed. We parked and Liam clambered out of the car. His idea of 'something tidier' was a blue tee shirt with a death's head on it, and black jeans, but at least neither garment had any holes.

We rang the doorbell and listened to the silence.

'Out,' Liam said. 'Or maybe he's gone deaf.'

The door opened as he spoke— Uncle George glared at him. We shuffled into the sitting room in some embarrassment. The settee and chairs looked like someone had taken a bicycle pump to them and blown them up into huge white balloons. Liam perched on the edge of a chair; I sat back on the sofa and found it giving way under me.

Uncle George was as smart as ever despite recently turning 71. His white hair was smoothed back over his head, contrasting with his dark blazer; I saw Liam's eyes stray to the jacket's shoulders, obviously looking for dandruff. I was certain there wouldn't be any. 'So,' George said. 'You're retired now, are you, Margaret?'

'It's my first day,' I agreed, 'And I'm already deep into researching the family history.'

His face hardened. 'I've no interest in that sort of thing. It's a hobby for old spinsters with nothing better to do.'

That hurt, but I said calmly, 'I was hoping you'd be able to identify some of the old family photographs.' I'd brought a handful with me, proffered them to George; he ignored them.

'What's the point? I daresay they're all dead and gone.'

Liam said unexpectedly, 'All the more reason to remember who they were then, surely?'

George looked him up and down. 'Your age, I'd already lived through a war,' he said contemptuously. 'You don't know how easy you have it.'

I calculated rapidly. If George had indeed known anything of the Second World War, he could only have been a baby. Maybe he meant the Falklands War? But he'd been managing the local branch of Woolworth's at the time.

'My life's not easy,' Liam said, mutinously. 'I work really hard . . .'

I seized the photo on top of my pile. 'Do you know who Aunt Pepper was?'

George stared at the photograph, very still for a moment. Then his eyes lifted to mine and he stood. 'Leave,' he said. 'Now!'

A minute later, we were back on the pavement, watching the front door close. George must have leant against it hard; it sounded loud and final.

Liam scowled. 'He doesn't know a thing about my life.'

I retreated to the end of the garden path, edged across a flowerbed to peer into the front room. George was standing with his back to the window, but he unmistakeably held a telephone to his ear. I headed back to the car. 'Come on.'

Liam dived into the passenger seat, grabbed his seat belt. 'Where to?'

'Uncle Philip,' I said grimly, 'But I'm willing to bet that was who George was ringing.'

So it wasn't much of a surprise when, three or four streets away, Philip didn't answer his door. The beige curtains were drawn back, the windows sparkled in the sunshine but no one, apparently, was home.

'He could have gone shopping,' Liam said.

'Philip has never gone shopping in his life,' I said tartly. This was ridiculous—why did neither of the brothers want to talk to me? Was there a skeleton in the family cupboard? I turned back for the car. 'Come on, Liam, there's still one person left who might know something—your mother.'

Liam winced.

*   *   *

Judith has one of those tall elegant Victorian town houses on the edge of the town centre. Liam hung back as I reached for the doorbell; I said, 'You can stay in the car if you like.'

He sighed. 'Thanks, but Mum'll only complain she never sees me.'

I said nothing, but I was remembering all the times Judith

11

had pulled the same guilt trip on me. I found my sister admirable—I really did. She'd brought up a son single-handedly after her husband died, while holding down a full-time job. I wasn't sure I could have done it. And Liam was a son to be proud of (though a little voice was suggesting that that might be *despite*, rather than *because of*, Judith's rather demanding standards). And now she'd started again with a second husband and a stepdaughter, and her career was flying higher every year. Yes, I admired her hugely—I just wished she didn't make me feel so inadequate.

I heard a scream somewhere inside the house. The petulant screech of an adolescent girl wanting her own way. Liam looked like he wanted to bolt back to the car but he grabbed the ornate railing which had somehow survived several world wars and shortages, and resolutely stayed put.

The door opened.

Judith was smartly dressed as always. A pencil-slim skirt, cashmere sweater and a neat bob of dark hair. She's always made me feel frumpish. Behind her, music suddenly blared. 'I really don't have any time at the moment, Madge,' she said, irritably. 'Perhaps you can make an appointment to see me tomorrow.'

An appointment? To see my own sister? Liam started to say something then wisely fell silent. Judith's eyes drifted to him. 'So you've decided to put in an appearance at long last, have you? I'm honoured.' She leant sideways slightly; Liam, correctly interpreting this as a command, planted a peck on her cheek.

'Well, come in if you must,' Judith said, and walked off into the house. She disappeared into the sitting room and the blare of the music subsided. She came out again and headed for the back of the house, into the kitchen—more of a conservatory really, with a huge glass wall letting in the sunshine from the garden.

'I'm surprised to find you in,' I said. 'I thought you'd be at work.'

Judith poured coffee from an expensive machine. 'I would be, if Tamsin didn't have toothache. I take it you do have a good reason for being here, Madge.'

Nothing like being made welcome. I appreciated anew why Liam had decided to move out, using a need to be closer to the university as an excuse to come and live with me.

'I was hoping for some information.' I looked down at the tiny expresso cup Judith presented me with. 'I've decided to research our family history.'

Judith arranged herself in one of the mahogany dining chairs at the kitchen table. 'I wish I had time for that sort of luxury.'

'I thought it might be fun.' I dragged out the chair opposite her;

she winced as it scraped across the tiled floor. I pushed the photographs across the table, Great Aunt Pepper on top of the pile. 'These were in that box of stuff Dad left when he died—the one we never got round to sorting out. Do you recognise any of them?'

She reached out a lethargic hand. 'Goodness, I can't be expected to remember all these people! They must have died years ago.'

'What about this one?' I pushed Great Aunt Pepper towards her.

She looked up at me from under her eyelids, a trick perfected since childhood—as if she was summing up all my faults and pondering on whether to mention them. I wondered if all sisters play such power games. 'I believe I ought to make it clear that Uncle George has just rung me.'

'What did he have to do that for?' Liam demanded indignantly.

'Why did he do that?' Judith

corrected automatically. 'Margaret, there's really no call to go round upsetting people with your latest fads. Uncle George is elderly. His health isn't good. He oughtn't to be bothered with things like this.'

'Most elderly people like talking about the past,' Liam protested.

'And why you have to drag Liam into this, I really don't know!'

'I volunteered,' he said.

I knew that tone of voice, that hint of petulance; Liam was reverting to his usual mode when dealing with his mother. The music blared from the sitting room again. Judith muttered and stalked out of the room, calling loudly, 'Tamsin!'

'Nothing changes,' Liam said morosely. 'She's always the same.'

My heart squeezed at the look on his face. Liam's always practical and he'd known the best thing to do was to leave home, but that didn't mean his mother's attitude didn't hurt.

The music faded again; Judith

strode back into the kitchen. 'Really, Madge, we don't all have time to waste.' She looked at my coffee as if I should have drunk it ages ago. 'But it's fortunate you came round. I need someone to look after Tamsin tomorrow. They're closing the school for some ridiculous reason. If you come round at 8 in the morning, I can get off to work as usual.'

I stared at her, unable to credit what I was hearing. 'You want me to babysit?'

'Well, it's not as if you've something better to do now you're retired,' she said indifferently.

The worst of it was that I was tempted to say yes. I didn't *want* to give in to her but I didn't have anything much to do—nothing that couldn't wait at any rate. After all, I was retired; Judith still had a job.

'Well . . . ' I started.

'You can't, Aunt Madge!' Liam, said with a whine. 'You promised to run me to Annie's house.'

I didn't have the slightest idea who Annie was; I stared at Liam blankly.

'You can't do it,' he said petulantly. 'I asked first. Come on, Aunt Madge. We've got to go.'

Judith glared, two spots of bright colour high on her pale cheeks. 'You can't do this, Margaret! I need you. Sisters ought to help each other out—'

Liam tugged at my arm as I hesitated. 'Come on! We're going to be late.' And he dragged me out of the kitchen into the narrow corridor to the front door.

The door of the sitting room opened as we hurried past; a young girl hesitated there. Twelve or thirteen years old, gorgeously blond and ridiculously made-up—and looking rather forlorn.

'Hi,' I said awkwardly.

She took refuge behind a long fall of hair and whisked herself back into the room. The music was turned up again.

18

'Tamsin!' Judith shouted.

We escaped to the safety of the car.

*   *   *

So that was day one of my retirement. Spent arguing with my whole family, and getting nowhere. Liam apologised for making up that ridiculous story to rescue me, but I was less than gracious. Feeling the pangs of conscience. After all, Judith *was* very busy and I wasn't.

Liam was subdued for the rest of the day, so when one of his friends from university rang up and asked him to come out for a beer, I was glad to see him cheer up.

'But I'll stay if you want me to,' he said, hovering at my elbow in the kitchen, where the old photographs were spread out on the table.

I frowned. In the year and a half since Liam came to stay with me, he's never felt the need to stay in to keep me company.

'Don't worry about me,' I said. 'I've loads of things to do.'

He grinned. 'I know you, Aunt Madge. You never give in once you get the bit between your teeth. You want to hunt around for Great Aunt Pepper, don't you?'

'I want to know why my interest in her provoked Uncle George into alerting the entire family,' I admitted. 'And I haven't looked at my emails all weekend.'

He went, grinning. I got out my laptop, then sat staring at it before switching on. It was three days since I left work, since that last tipsy lunch with the girls, that farewell present and the CEO's rather too complimentary farewell speech. And the promise they had all made to keep in touch. Particularly about the meeting with the Music Festival directors today.

I didn't know whether I wanted to know what had happened or not.

20

I switched on, logged into my email. Apart from the usual spam, the in-box was empty.

I made coffee. Perhaps it was for the best. A clean break. After all, there was so much I wanted to do. That long-anticipated cruise, redecorating the house, the family history. And lots more beside. Even if my plans did seem a little indulgent, when Judith was run off her feet . . .

Resolutely, to prevent myself ringing Judith, I logged on to one of the several genealogy sites I'd taken out a subscription to and spent an hour or two sorting out my parents' details: birth, marriage and death. Then my maternal grandparents, whom I'd known well; it all fell into place with gratifying ease.

Obviously, it couldn't last. My father's side was much trickier; his mother had died when she gave birth to the last of her four children and I didn't even know her first name.

Where to start?

The phone rang.

The voice on the other end was male and young, or youngish—he sounded in his thirties, as near as I could tell. He said, apologetically, 'I'm afraid you probably won't remember me. I'm Martin Williams —Jane's stepson.'

It took me a moment before I remembered that Aunt Jane— George and Philip's sister—had married an American widower with a young son. 'Martin! Goodness, I haven't seen you since you were, oh, five years old!'

'That's right.' He was making an effort to sound relaxed, I thought, but there was something tense in his voice. 'I was wondering if we could meet.'

Well, I'd been wanting to sort out the family history—maybe Martin could help. He might even have photographs belonging to Aunt Jane.

'Tomorrow,' he said. 'For lunch?'

That sense of unease was intensifying and I had a feeling I knew why. 'Was there something you particularly wanted to talk about?'

The tiniest of pauses. 'Uncle George rang me. He said you were asking about Great Aunt Pepper.' He hesitated, then plunged on, as if he knew it was now or never. 'I think there was something suspicious about her death. I think she was murdered.'

2

I went out the next morning still feeling horribly guilty about not babysitting for my sister Judith. She'd rung me up at nine to tell me she'd been unable to find someone and was therefore having to work from home—she was almost shouting to make herself heard over the music in the background. She'd left a moment or two for my conscience to prompt me into giving in, but I took refuge in my lunch appointment. I had the distinct impression she didn't believe I had any such meeting—she rang off very abruptly.

I'd arranged to meet my step cousin, Martin Williams, in the restaurant on the second floor of John Lewis but didn't have the slightest idea how I'd recognise him. He'd been a little boy when his parents divorced and his father had taken him back to America; he'd been brought up in the States, therefore, and I'd had the impression that Aunt Jane had had nothing more to do with her ex-husband and stepson. I certainly hadn't seen Martin, or a photograph of him, since he was a toddler. Given he'd probably not seen a photograph of me either, I had a vision of the two of us wandering around John Lewis forlornly in search of each other.

The restaurant was beginning to fill up as I went in. There were three men sitting on their own: an elderly man who was impatiently signalling to his wife in the queue; a young man in a smart suit, trying to juggle a mobile between ear and shoulder as he typed on his laptop; and chewed ferociously on gum; and a third man, at a table by the window. Surely *he* couldn't be Martin; he didn't look as if he belonged in our family, even tangentially. Much too glamorous.

He stood and raised an uncertain

hand in greeting. A man in his very late thirties, with an unmistakeable air of cosmopolitan sophistication. A long coat over a stylish suit, light blue shirt and red tie. Dark hair, just a trace long, in elegant disarray. An open, lean face with the uncertain beginnings of a smile. Blue eyes. Handsome and self-assured. The word Liam would have used was *cool*.

I found myself wishing I was twenty years younger. Ridiculous!

We shook hands. He said, 'I took the liberty of getting you a coffee— if you prefer something else . . .?' He had a light voice with just the hint of a transatlantic drawl.

'Coffee's fine,' I said, sitting down opposite him. 'I'm glad to meet you at last. Even though we're not strictly related.'

'Is there a proper word for step-cousins?' He smiled slightly, stirred his black coffee. 'All the same, your family is all I have. There's no one on my father's side—he was an only child.'

'How is he?'

He glanced down at his coffee briefly. 'He died last year.' He looked up again reassuringly. 'Don't feel guilty at not knowing. He'd been ill a long time and I was glad to see him at peace.' He said awkwardly, 'You must be thinking me crazy—talking of Aunt Pepper being murdered.'

'I was startled,' I admitted. I sipped at my coffee—it was smooth and dark. Just like Martin. 'I should explain that I fell into all this by accident, just yesterday, when I decided to investigate the family history. I had no idea my uncles would object so violently.' I pushed the photograph of Great Aunt Pepper across the table to him. 'Have you seen this before?'

He shook his head. 'She looks a real dragon.' He slid the photo back towards me. 'The more I think about this, the more I wonder if I've exaggerated everything. Only Uncle George was so insistent I shouldn't talk to you, that I began to wonder if it wasn't all true after all.' He gave me a gorgeous smile. 'He was so very offensive—and I've never been good at doing what I'm told.'

I sipped my coffee, trying to mitigate the effect of that smile. 'Funnily enough, Uncle George has the same effect on me. It wouldn't have been so bad if he'd given me an explanation for his behaviour. What makes you think there was something untoward about Great Aunt Pepper's death?'

'All I know is what my stepmother told me, on her deathbed—'

He started to tell me the story, relating it in a level, even tone which told me he must have gone over it in his mind several times before coming here. Three years ago, when Aunt Jane had been dying of breast cancer, Martin had come over from New York to see her. She'd sent for

28

him, apparently, but forgotten she'd done so. I got the impression that Aunt Jane had been confused—she'd called Martin by his father's name, ranted and raved, and raked over arguments that were decades old and unimportant even when they were new. But Martin insisted she'd been lucid when talking about Great Aunt Pepper.

'She told me how Aunt Pepper came to live with them when their mother died, to look after them. This was at the beginning of the 1950s. According to my stepmother, it was pretty much war in the household. The kids hated Aunt Pepper, and she hated them, but their father insisted on having her there. She kept the household pretty much in line, I guess.'

'Do you know her name? She can't have been christened Pepper, surely.'

'Philippa,' he said. 'Pippa. Pepper was a nickname and it stuck.'

Maybe one of the children hadn't

mispronounced *Pippa*—that's how these things usually start.

'Anyway,' he said, shifting slightly to allow a woman with a pushchair to manoeuvre past. 'Apparently, she died when my stepmother was 16, which would make it 1966. Aunt Pepper was in her early sixties, apparently.'

I glanced at the photograph. Great Aunt Pepper looked seventy years old at least, with her unflattering clothes, and stiff pose. People grew older earlier in those days, I supposed.

'She evidently went for a walk one night, in the dark, in wind and rain, and was found the next morning, face down in a ditch at the side of the road. Drowned.'

Poor Aunt Pepper. An ignominious dirty little death. 'It wasn't an accident?'

'The inquest decided it was. Or so my stepmother said. There was definitely something odd about it.

Mom had the affair on her mind the whole time, the last week of her life. She kept mentioning it. She kept saying: *She didn't struggle. It was as if she wanted to die.* All the time, she kept going over it. Again and again.'

He lifted his gaze to mine, said, 'I know what you're thinking.'

'Do you?' I asked levelly.

'I didn't particularly like my stepmother,' he admitted. 'She treated my father very badly. Of course, I lived with him, I had his side of the story and not hers—I admit that. But I don't want to accuse her of murder. Especially not when she's not around to defend herself. I'd not bring the whole matter up again if I thought she'd done it. What would be the point when she's dead? Only—'

He broke off, took a deep breath in. 'The way my stepmother told it, she wasn't alone. Uncle George and Uncle Philip were there as well.'

'Nice lunch?' Liam asked. He'd obviously had a good day with his friends and was in high spirits.

I reddened, remembering Martin's blue eyes and attractive Transatlantic accent . . . 'Interesting,' I said lightly.

Liam peered at me suspiciously. 'Just interesting?'

'Something to eat? I've a lasagne in the oven.'

'Wow!' He bolted for the cutlery drawer, grabbed mats for the table. 'You're going to have to clear that laptop from the table. Come on, what's the latest on GAP?'

'GAP?'

'Great Aunt Pepper.'

I shifted the laptop, let him lay the table. 'As a matter of fact, I could do with a fresh mind on the subject. Listen and concentrate—this gets complicated. Are you ready?'

He arranged cutlery, reached for serviettes. 'I'm listening. Do you want me to take notes?'

'No, thank you—I'm not so old yet that my memory's going. I've only been retired a day and a half. Your grandfather—my father—had two brothers, George and Philip, and a sister, Jane. Their mother died when Jane was born, so Great Aunt Pepper was brought in to look after them. She was their mother's sister— her name was Philippa Mary Alice Brownlow.'

'That's a mouthful,' Liam said, taking a look at the table to make sure that he had put everything out. 'I shall continue to call her GAP.'

'Your grandfather was much older than the others and was away at university so he isn't involved in any of this. The others were all in the house on the crucial night: 10th March, 1966. It was a wet and windy night, apparently, and there'd been a huge argument. Great Aunt Pepper said she knew when she wasn't wanted, packed a bag and walked out.'

Liam frowned. 'Martin what's-his-name told you all this?'

'No. I checked the local papers and found the report of the inquest.' I patted the laptop. 'Amazing what's online nowadays. Everyone else was furious too, according to the evidence, and they all went to bed in a huff. They said they'd thought she'd gone for the bus. It wasn't until the following day that the postman discovered her body in a ditch less than 200 yards from the house. She'd drowned.'

'Nasty.' Liam wrinkled up his nose. 'Accidental death?'

'That's what the coroner said.'

His gaze went very still. He said, 'Is that what Martin said?'

The smell of the lasagne was wafting through the kitchen making my stomach growl. 'I'm not sure how reliable Martin's story is.'

'So he said something else, right?'

'He only knows what he was told

by his stepmother—Aunt Jane—
when she was dying. And she wasn't
always lucid.'

'So what did she say?'

'I really don't think—'

'Aunt Madge!' he said
exasperated. 'Uncle George was
phoning round telling everyone not
to talk to us within seconds of us
leaving him! *He* doesn't think it was
straightforward!'

I had to agree that George's
reaction—his over-reaction—
was suspicious. 'Martin says his
stepmother implied that Great Aunt
Pepper was murdered.'

'Wow!' Liam said, grinning. 'I
mean—' He tried to quell the grin.
'Who did the dreadful deed?'

'Liam, this is serious!'

He looked chastened. 'Yes, I
know. It's just—' He bit his lip. The
grin was trying to surface again. 'It
was over half a century ago!'

'Yes.' I sighed. Half a century ago,
and all I had to go on was Martin's

tale of Aunt Jane's ramblings and a hint in the newspaper accounts that the police had not been entirely happy with the coroner's decision. What good could it do to rake all this up again now? 'Let's have the lasagne.'

Steam billowed from the oven as I took the dish out, and with it the smell of rich meat and tomato, and herbs. 'Wow,' Liam said again and we sat down to eat.

He'd had some adventures of his own during the day—one of his university chums had had a huge argument with her landlord over whether she could stay in the property until Congregations and the conferring of her degree. Annoyed, she'd moved out and was sleeping on someone else's floor, and now the landlord was refusing to return her deposit on the property. Liam and a couple of others had gone round to lend her moral support, and then they'd all gone off to the police station to complain about her treatment.

I sat listening idly, still half thinking of Martin. It had been curiously pleasant to have Liam staying the last year or so; sometimes I'd even caught myself imagining that he was *my* son. But he'd be off any day now. He'd get his results and look for a job, find a 'significant other', maybe. It was as if I'd just borrowed him for a while . . .

I'd miss him.

The phone rang. Liam and I both jumped. 'Bet that's mum,' Liam said. 'She probably wants you to babysit Tamsin again. Tell her you've got to take me to a party.'

'You'll be getting a terrible reputation,' I joked. Across the kitchen, the mobile phone was almost dancing on the smooth surface of the work surface, its screen brightly lit. I checked caller ID. 'It's Uncle Philip.'

'Uh-ho,' Liam said. I answered

the call but Philip didn't give me a chance to speak.

'Margaret,' he said imperiously. 'We need to talk. Now.'

'About Great Aunt Pepper?'

'Now, Margaret,' he said. The doorbell rang.

When I opened the door, Philip was standing on the step in rain I hadn't known had started, looking distinctly damp and jaundiced. I called to Liam to make some coffee and took Philip through into the kitchen.

Philip is the brother who came between George and Jane; he's worn well—his hair is still largely dark and he's not put on weight, unlike his brother. He glanced about the kitchen, looking disapprovingly at the dirty dishes Liam had just piled on the drainer.

'I've been talking to George,' he said, without preamble. 'You've got to stop this nonsense, Margaret.'

I poured out coffee, gestured him

to a seat at the table, and sat down opposite him. 'I've been trying to, certainly.'

'About that woman.' He turned up his nose, hopefully at the thought of Great Aunt Pepper, rather than at the coffee.

'You didn't like her?'

'She breezed in—took everything over!'

'Presumably that's what your father wanted—someone to run the house and look after the children.'

'She was sour,' he said. 'Always complaining, always blaming people for things *she'd* done. Setting one person against another!' Another wrinkle of his nose. 'Old spinster.' He laughed. 'No one would have her. You should have heard what she had to say about men!'

'Was Jane her favourite then?'

He settled more comfortably in the hard chair, looking relieved. Maybe he'd anticipated a fight. 'Not a bit of it—she hated her. She was a pretty little thing, Jane, could get what she wanted out of everybody. Except Great Aunt Pepper.'

'Who christened her that?'

He shrugged. 'Can't remember now. Never used it to her face, mind. She had a damn hard slap.'

Liam paused in the act of loading the dishwasher. 'Perhaps you deserved it.'

Uncle Philip flared up at once. 'In my day, young man, you would have been the first in line for punishment!'

Liam rolled his eyes. I was thinking that no one could have been in any doubt that Philip and George were brothers; they had the same air about them, the same attitudes.

'I've been reading the papers,' I intervened. 'Aunt Pepper drowned in a ditch after an argument one night. The coroner said it was accidental death but the police comments suggest they weren't entirely convinced.'

Philip nodded. 'She didn't

confine her arguments to us, you see. She had a go at everyone in the neighbourhood one time or another. According to her, the butcher gave short weight, the baker's buns were always stale, the greengrocer gave her the old fruit. Wasn't a soul in the neighbourhood that liked her.'

'So you think the baker or the butcher might have pushed her into the ditch?'

'Oh, not deliberately!' Philip took a great gulp of the coffee. 'It was a dreadful night, remember, could hardly see an inch in front of your face. Supposing one of them came along in his van, driving a bit fast maybe, she had to jump out of the way, or maybe he caught her, and didn't bother to stop? Maybe he never even knew.'

'A kind of accident, then?'

Maybe there was something in my voice, a hint of scepticism. He looked at me sharply. 'What's the point in bringing it all up again?'

'George asked much the same thing.'

'And he's damn right. The woman's dead and—'

'And?' I prompted as he hesitated.

'No. Nothing!' he said. 'We're all getting old, Margaret. Won't be long until we're all gone.'

'Very cheerful,' Liam said.

'Leave it be, I say. Nothing to be gained from dragging it all out into the open again.'

'There is, if a murderer is still hanging around, unpunished.'

'There's all sorts of punishment,' he said bitterly, and for a brief moment I seemed to catch sight of the real man beneath the bluster. He hesitated again. 'Look if you knew the—the *malefactor*—was dead, would you leave it then?'

Now it was my turn to pause. 'Well—'

He put the coffee cup down with a snap and leant towards me. 'It's all over, Margaret. Long since dealt with.'

'Martin Williams doesn't think so.'

He frowned. 'Is that Jane's stepson? He's over here?'

'Some sort of legal matter over Aunt Jane's property, I think he said. He's seen George. He's staying at the Cavendish.'

Philip laughed sourly. 'Plenty of money then. Americans!'

He pushed back his chair and stood up, buttoning up his coat. 'Well, must get going. Back out into the rain, eh? No, don't worry about seeing me out. Drop the subject, Margaret. You don't want to get on George's bad side, do you?"

'I don't give a fig about Uncle George's opinion,' I said. 'And I'm not sure I *can* drop it.'

His temper snapped suddenly. He pushed the chair in to the table with an angry flourish. 'Women!' he said furiously, and stalked out.

*   *   *

Liam watched him through the hall, until the front door shut with a sharp click. 'He's got it bad, hasn't he?' He frowned. That crack about what you would do if the murderer was dead— Do you think he was trying to say *Aunt Jane* did it? That would tie in with what Martin told you, wouldn't it?'

I leant back in the hard chair, trying to make sense of it all. 'I'm beginning to think there's no point in pursuing the matter. At this late date, there's no way I'm going to get evidence one way or another—it's all pure speculation. Maybe I ought just to fill Philippa Brownlow in on the family tree and leave it at that.'

Liam started to giggle.

'Now what's the matter?' I demanded crossly.

'Your face, Aunt Madge! You can't bear the thought of not knowing the answer!'

I sighed. He was right. For the

first time, I realised I hadn't thought about work all day. About the office, and who was or wasn't finishing off the things I'd started, and whether there was any point in doing anything any more. That dreadful feeling of lethargy that had threatened me yesterday morning had been conspicuous by its absence.

'I can't see it can do any harm investigating,' I said at last. 'Not if I keep the answer to myself.'

'*Our*selves,' Liam corrected. 'I'm not going to be left out of this, Aunt Madge. I'm enjoying this! Do you think I'd be any good as a private detective? That would be fun, following people around all day, ferreting out mysteries . . .'

'Getting arrested for phone-hacking. . .' I murmured.

On cue, my mobile rang again. No caller ID. And an unknown number. Another unknown male voice.

'Mrs Andrews?'

'*Ms* Andrews,' I said.

'I'm Detective Constable Gupta. Do you know a Martin Williams?'

My knees went weak. I put out a hand to grasp the side of the work surface. Liam said, 'What's wrong?'

'I'm afraid,' the detective constable said, 'there's been an accident . . .'

3

I'd not been in Accident and Emergency for years and it was just as unpleasant as I remembered. It was crowded, Liam's nose was wrinkled at the smell of blood and antiseptic from the moment we walked in, and there was the constant noise of coughing, and children grizzling.

The nurse on duty greeted us with relief when she realised we weren't yet more patients and ushered us through into a narrow, echoing corridor. A swish of a curtain and we were looking at Martin, dressed in blood-stained shirt and trousers, sitting on the edge of a bed and arguing with a doctor. Martin was obviously intent on discharging himself, the doctor was trying to insist he stayed in overnight for observation.

Liam's eyes widened as he saw the thick bandage on Martin's head; I said involuntarily, 'What on earth happened?'

'At last!' Martin said, 'The voice of sanity! Madge, do you have your car with you? Can you run me back to my hotel?'

'Course we can,' Liam said brightly, and introduced himself. 'No problem.'

'None at all,' I agreed. 'If you're sure you should be leaving here.'

'Yes,' Martin said. 'No,' the doctor said at the same time.

The doctor talked about tests, then about possible repercussions, then about paperwork. Then about the detective wanting to ask some questions. Martin ignored all of it, grabbed his jacket and headed for the door. I held onto him as he swayed slightly, but he managed a convincingly independent walk down the corridor.

In the car, he sank back as Liam

scrambled in behind me. 'I'm grateful for your help. I hope you don't mind me giving the police your number?'

'Not at all,' I said, and repeated. 'What happened?'

He turned his head on the headrest. 'I was crossing the street when a car came round the corner and hit me. Just brushed me—I managed to get myself out of the way but tripped and fell. Hit my head on the sidewalk.' His mouth twisted into a wry smile. 'The doctor thinks I forgot which country I was in and looked the wrong way before crossing the street.'

'Did you?'

He shook his head, winced. 'It's not exactly my first time abroad. I may sound American but I've visited over here almost every year.'

'Still—if you were preoccupied . . .'

'No,' he said, firmly. 'Madge, do you mind if we don't talk now? My head's pounding. I'd really much rather discuss this in the morning.'

I started the engine. 'Of course.' He closed his eyes. I cast a glance back at Liam—he was looking thoughtful.

Martin's hotel was no doubt very good but given the doctor's reservations about discharging him, I didn't think it wise he should be on his own. I drove instead to my own house, pondering on what had happened. It could have been a simple hit and run, of course, or Martin really had had a moment of inattention . . .

'Liam,' I said softly, to avoid disturbing Martin. 'Ring Uncle George, will you? And Uncle Philip.'

He stared at me for a moment, then started thumbing away at his mobile. After a while, he whispered, 'No answer from either of them.'

'Try your mother.'

'Must I?' He groaned, but put the mobile to his ear. After a moment, I heard him say, 'Is Mum in?' A pause.

'You on your own? No, I'm not . . .
Tamsin, I simply . . . Yeah, yeah . . .
Well, thanks a lot!'

He pushed the mobile back into
his pocket. 'That girl's impossible!'

'Judith's not in?'

'Nope.'

'Then who's looking after
Tamsin?'

'Half a dozen of her friends, by the
sound of it.'

'Music?'

'And shrieking.'

'Try Judith's mobile.'

'Haven't got the number,' he said.
'She changed it last week and said
she wouldn't give me the number or
I'd only bother her when she didn't
want it.'

I made a mental note to have some
strong words with my sister.

*   *   *

Half an hour later, Martin was in the
guest room, already asleep under

the incongruously pink duvet. He'd managed a cup of hot chocolate, half a biscuit and two painkillers before admitting defeat and struggling upstairs with our help. After a suitable period, I sent Liam in to pick up his clothing and checked it out in the kitchen. The collar of the shirt was bloodstained and the suit jacket slightly torn on one elbow but otherwise it wasn't too bad.

Liam watched me stuff the shirt in the washing machine. 'Uncle George didn't answer, Uncle Philip didn't answer, Mum didn't answer.'

'At least we know Tamsin's in the clear,' I said, flippantly.

'They all have cars, Aunt Madge.'

I straightened up. Liam was looking unusually sombre.

'It could have been an accident,' I pointed out.

'Do you believe that?'

I twirled the knobs of the machine, set it running. 'No,' I admitted and turned to make us both hot chocolate. 'But I don't see *why* anyone should try and hurt Martin.'

'The murderer is afraid he'll tell us vital information about the death of Great Aunt Pepper!'

'But if they know about Martin, they should know I'd already talked to him,' I pointed out.

'There might be more he isn't telling us,' Liam said ghoulishly. 'Stuff he doesn't know he knows. Is he staying long?'

'As long as he wants,' I said.

Liam grinned; I said with a touch of defiance, 'I like having people around.'

I stirred milk into the chocolate. It *was* nice. Too nice, in fact. First Liam, now Martin. I'd lived on my own so long, I'd thought I'd resent having someone else around; I thought I'd be driven mad by mess and late nights and unwashed dishes and all the rest of it. But Liam had turned out to be more house-trained than I was, and within two weeks was washing up without being asked and even putting doing his own washing. However bad my relations with my sister Judith, and however harsh I thought her with Liam sometimes, I had to admit she'd brought him up well.

But Liam would no doubt soon be out of the house and getting his own flat. He'd already mentioned a friend who wanted to share rent on a house across town. And then it would be quiet again. Of course, it had never bothered me before, but then I'd had a job to go out to . . .

*   *   *

Detective Gupta came round next morning, about 10 o'clock. Liam had gone out for coffee with friends, and Martin had only just got up. The detective was a middle-aged man with a comfortable beer paunch; he questioned Martin at length but it was clear what he thought even though he didn't specifically say so. Martin had been the victim of an accident caused a motorist silly enough not to stop. Probably a drink driver.

He went, and Martin finished the coffee he was sipping, and shifted uneasily. 'I'd better go.'

I shook my head. 'Don't feel obliged to.'

'I'm inconveniencing you dreadfully.'

'No, it's good to have company.'

He gave me that lovely smile. 'Yes, I agree. Living alone can be tedious.'

'There isn't a Mrs Williams, then?' The words were out before I could stop them; I cringed at the intrusiveness of them. But Martin didn't seem annoyed.

'There was once but it didn't last long.' He looked at me, flushed, looked away. 'We were both too young.'

'American?'

He nodded. 'We somehow didn't

have the knack of conversation. It was all—*pass the salt, what would you like for dinner, how did work go today*—that sort of thing. That and sex.'

'That doesn't necessarily sound too bad,' I said. 'I only ever had two serious relationships, when I was a great deal younger. Both were with men older than myself and looking for an attractive trophy relationship. The trouble is, I'm getting to the stage where there aren't many men older than me.'

Martin was frowning. 'You have to be kidding me, right? You're not that old.'

'I retired yesterday—though it was early retirement admittedly.'

He grinned. 'There are days when I wish I could retire. I got the boss from hell.'

'Oh, I've had a good few of those,' I said. And the next thing I knew we were swapping stories about impossible executives and worse supervisors, and falling into giggles over stories I'd only ever been appalled by before.

The doorbell rang. Martin looked at his watch, startled. 'It's nearly lunchtime.'

'Good heavens!' I glanced at the coffee pot—I'd filled it two or three times and it was empty again. 'I'd no idea.' The doorbell rang again. 'I'll just get that.'

He got up. 'I'd better be getting back to my hotel.'

A sudden wave of disappointment overtook me. 'Yes,' I said. 'Yes. I suppose so.'

We went together to the door. I opened it to see Judith, hands full of plastic bags. She looked surprised to see Martin; I offered up silent thanks that she'd not come around breakfast time—she would certainly have drawn the wrong conclusions.

'Martin—this is my sister Judith. Judith, this is Martin—Aunt Jane's stepson.'

She stared at him. Her hair was unusually tousled, her blouse slightly crumpled as if she'd put on yesterday's clothes again. I felt a pang of conscience. Looking after a husband and stepchild, *and* doing a full-time job was not exactly a bed of roses.

'I thought you lived in America,' she said. She probably didn't intend to make it sound so accusing.

'I do.' Martin gave her one of his smiling glances; she didn't even seem to notice. 'And I've obviously changed a lot since we last saw each other—given I was only a few years old. I have some old pictures of you. From when you were staying with my mother and her family. You were ill, I think.'

'No,' she corrected, 'that was Madge.'

'I don't remember being ill.'

'You had measles.' She held out a hand to Martin. 'Don't let me keep you.'

He looked disconcerted, but said smilingly, 'Of course not.' He hesitated—I had the impression he was about to say something but changed his mind. He said, 'The old photos were my father's—they're on my laptop. I'll check them out to see if there's anything that might interest you.'

Ridiculous to feel so pleased that he'd get back to me. I said something about being grateful; we muttered some conventional platitudes then he was off down the street, striding out confidently. He didn't look back.

Judith had already pushed past me; when I went back in, she was in the kitchen, dumping the carrier bags on the table.

'I don't remember having measles,' I said.

'You were eight, I was seven,' she said briskly. She gestured at the bags. 'I've been meaning to throw this lot out for years but you might as well have them.'

She pushed the bags towards me; I took the first, delved in and pulled out an old bible in a black leather cover; the pages were edged with gold and the colour illustrations were in an old-fashioned, slightly sentimental style. Inside the front cover, in flowing Victorian-style handwriting, it said: *presented to our dear son, Malcolm, on his tenth birthday. Mummy and Daddy.*

I stared. 'This is Dad's bible!'

Judith started pulling things out of the other bags: bundles of letters, photograph albums, boxes that had clearly once held chocolates but which now had perished rubber bands barely keeping them closed.

'Is this is the stuff Dad asked us to store when he moved from the house into the bungalow after mum's death?'

'He said he'd go through it and decide what to throw out and what to keep,' Judith said sourly, 'but he never did.' She fingered a black and white photograph with some contempt, handed it across to me. It was of mum, dad, Judith and me—I'd been about six, Judith five. I'd forgotten we'd had pigtails—we both looked absolutely dreadful. I giggled.

'It's not that bad,' Judith said sharply.

'Sorry, I've just been swapping silly stories with Martin.'

She stared at me. 'You really are odd this morning.'

'Coffee?' I suggested, thinking that if I drank another cup I'd probably start swimming.

She nodded, sat down abruptly, as I filled the kettle again. 'I knew Great Aunt Pepper.'

She said it with such emphasis that I suddenly realised this was why she had come—to tell me this story. I plugged the kettle in, sat down at the table with her. 'While I had the measles?'

'They packed me off to live with

the others while mum nursed you. She said she *couldn't be doing with me hanging around* while she was busy.'

I winced at the bitterness in her tone.

'I was only seven years old,' she said, 'but I remember it vividly. Dad was off at university but the others were all there—Uncle George and Uncle Philip, and Aunt Jane. She was only sixteen and she was mad with me all the time. People expected she would look after me— being a girl, I suppose—and she hated not being able to go out with her friends.'

'Grandfather must have been there too, and Great Aunt Pepper.'

She nodded. 'I don't remember Grandfather very well, he was always out at work. I remember Great Aunt Pepper, though.' She said, with an outburst of bitterness, 'She was a *horrible* old woman! Always saying nasty things, and carrying tales, and lying about people. We all hated her.'

I wondered if Great Aunt Pepper had been horrible *because* people hated her. If she wasn't welcome, it must have been a great temptation to live up to her reputation.

'Do you remember the day she died?'

Judith looked up, looked around the kitchen. 'Where's that coffee?'

I got up, made two mugsful and searched out the shortbread biscuits. Judith supped the coffee daintily. 'The weather was dreadful—it rained all day, and we had to stay in. Uncle George and Uncle Philip played cards. I was bored and ate too much cake. Aunt Jane and Aunt Pepper argued *all* day, hour after hour. Aunt Jane wanted to go out with her boyfriend, but Aunt Pepper wouldn't let her. She was jealous, that's what it was. Just because no one had ever been interested in her.'

I thought she'd remembered a

surprisingly large amount—I didn't remember much from when I was seven. 'Do you recall Aunt Pepper leaving the house?'

She shook her head. 'I was probably in bed. I wasn't even told she was dead, or about the inquest or anything like that.'

'All that would probably have been kept from a child so young.'

She sat up straighter. 'Margaret, you can have no idea how nasty that woman was, or what it was like living with her, but you seem to have started on a crusade to find out what happened to her. I really don't understand what you hope to gain. Draw up our family tree by all means, if it gives you something to do, but to make so much from an old woman's death! Really, this is sensationalism of the worst kind!'

I curbed my irritation. 'Uncle George did act very oddly,' I pointed out. 'He warned everyone off talking to me about her. If there was ever anything guaranteed to rouse my interest, that was it!'

'Uncle George is a very private man,' she said. 'You know that.'

'Yes,' I agreed. 'And I know why too.'

She glared. 'What do you mean by that?'

'I mean, he seems to have had affairs with half the married women in town! There are definitely some husbands he wouldn't want to face on a dark night.'

'Margaret!' Judith sounded scandalised. She gathered herself together again. 'I want you to promise me you'll give up this silly obsession with Great Aunt Pepper. It's silly—you're just setting the entire family at odds.'

I pondered whether to tell her about Martin's *accident* last night. She had apparently not even noticed the bandage on his temple. I decided against it—she would only say I was making too much of it.

She gestured wildly, suddenly close to tears. 'Oh, *Madge*—how did this happen?'

I was startled—I'd never seen her upset before. Angry, yes, but in tears, never. Judith was someone who took the world by the scruff of the neck and *did something* if she didn't like the way things were turning out. Always so capable.

'How did we all come to be like this?' She pushed back her chair, stood up, covering her mouth with her hand. 'We're all at each other's throats! Uncle George keeps ringing me to complain, Uncle Philip accosts me in the street, and Tamsin keeps on and on and *on* with that music. And now Liam won't talk to me!'

'Liam?' I said, foundering. Acutely uncomfortable. What was I to do or say? I didn't have the least idea. This was so unexpected. 'Liam's not annoyed with you, or upset.'

'He rang me,' Judith said angrily. 'Told me I wasn't to be rude to you.'

I was astonished. Liam had rung her to defend me? 'Well, you know what kids are like,' I said, embarrassed. 'He'll come round. And Tamsin's probably just going through an awkward phase . . .'

She shook her head. Her voice cracked. She said, 'I don't *want* to live like this.' She lifted her eyes to mine. 'It's *her* fault. Great Aunt Pepper.' Her mouth twisted bitterly. 'That's when it started. She set everyone against everyone else. She kept telling me people were envious of me, that they were unfair to me, that I wasn't loved as much as you were . . .'

It was all I could do to stop myself wincing. I hadn't known that Great Aunt Pepper had said all that, but I did known Judith thought those things. I'd lost track of the number of times she'd told me our parents loved me best because I was older, or how I always got the best presents, how everyone made allowances for me.

She dropped her hands, took a deep breath, straightened. Back to the old Judith, in control, in charge. She waved her hand at the bags. 'You can keep all this. Or throw it out if you like. I don't want it back, it's just cluttering up the loft. But get some sense, Margaret! Great Aunt Pepper was just a nasty old woman who made people's lives a misery. Don't resurrect her now to make more mischief!'

And she stooped to pick up her handbag, and strode out into the hall.

She jerked open the front door. Liam was standing directly outside, hand raised with the key in it. He reddened. 'Hi, mum.'

Judith swept past him to her car parked at the kerb. Liam winced.

'Don't mind your mother,' I said. 'We've just had a sisterly spat. I thought you were going to spend the day with your university friends.'

Liam shook his head, came in and pushed the front door to. 'I've been doing some investigations!'

I stared in alarm. 'Liam, you haven't . . .'

'No one saw me,' he said, soothingly. 'But I've found out something *very* interesting. You'll never guess what Uncle Philip did this morning!'

I was just realising how tired I was. Talking to Judith is tiring at the best of times, and today was definitely not that. 'I'm not in the mood for riddles, Liam.'

'But this is important,' he said, and suddenly swallowed. 'Uncle Philip took his car into the garage this morning—there's loads of damage to the front passenger wing.'

4

Martin sounded tired when I rang—I wondered if his head was still aching. But his voice lifted when he realised who I was. 'Madge!' he said in that delightful Transatlantic accent. 'I was just thinking of you.'

I wanted to be flattered; I said cautiously, 'It was a pleasant thought, I hope.'

'I was wondering—'

'Yes?'

'Well, I have to go back to the States on Saturday—'

In the silence that followed, I tried desperately to think of something to say. I couldn't. *Really, Madge— you're a fifty four-year old woman—a* retired *woman and you're making eyes at a man fifteen years younger than you. You're making a fool of yourself* . . .

'I was wondering if you'd care to

have dinner with me,' he said.

I understood—he thought he owed me something for the help I'd given him last night. Gratitude somehow was worse than indifference.

'Nonsense,' I said briskly. 'There's no need.'

'I want to.' He hesitated. 'I was thinking—I mean—I was hoping . . .' I heard him take a deep breath. 'I'm sorry, I've never been any good at this sort of thing. You must think me a callow idiot, but I was hoping we could go somewhere—' He said in a more determined fashion, 'Somewhere *romantic.*'

I was cast adrift. Really, this was ridiculous. I knew what Judith would say—she'd be immediately suspicious. *You haven't given him reason to suspect you have money, have you?*

'Hello?' he said at the other end of the line. 'Are you still there?'

And suddenly I didn't care. If

it turned out he was just after my money—which was little enough, for heaven's sake!—so be it.

'I'd love to,' I said brightly. 'Tonight?'

He laughed shakily. 'I saw this great restaurant on the main street, next to the bank. Do you like Italian?'

'I love it,' I said. 'How about seven o'clock?'

Someone moved behind me. I glanced round. Liam was standing in the kitchen door, grinning broadly. I turned my back on him. 'As a matter of fact,' I said to Martin, 'I was calling about the accident. You didn't see what colour the car was, did you?'

'Best I could tell the cops was that it was very pale,' he said ruefully. 'Looked kind of green to me. Does that mean anything to you?'

'It might.'

'Madge,' he said. 'Don't do anything silly, will you? Whatever

72

the cops say, it *wasn't* an accident. I don't want you to get caught up in something dangerous.' He swore. 'The woman's fifty years dead—who can be so determined to make sure her killer isn't found? It's history!'

Family history. I wished I'd left well alone, that I'd never seen Aunt Pepper's photograph. 'I think you should stay in your hotel.'

'I was planning on it anyway,' he said. 'Me, my pounding head and my laptop. I told you I got all my father's photographs on it? He had some very old pictures my mother gave him—I've been wondering if there was one of the great aunt in there.'

'Let me know if you find anything,' I said lightly.

I rang off, put the phone down, walked past Liam to put the kettle on.

'That was a date, right?' Liam said, still grinning. 'You're going out with Martin?'

'We're just going to discuss family

history,' I said firmly.

'You could go to America with him! Could you pick somewhere really good to live, like New York or LA? I could come and visit you!' He bounded over and gave me a big hug. 'You deserve it, Aunt Madge! You've helped me so much!'

I blinked. '*I* have?'

'I've *so* much more confidence. I don't get scared by girls any more!'

I'd noticed. 'That's what university's done for you.'

'No, no, it was you. I wish you'd been my mother—you never nag me.'

'I don't see why I should.' The kettle boiled; I made coffee to cover up my embarrassment. 'You make your bed, put your socks in the laundry basket and wash up—what more could anyone want?'

Liam said darkly, 'You wouldn't believe it. Mum has so many rules and she never fails to point out when I break them! Did Martin recognise the car?'

'He thought it might be pale green.'

'Jackpot!' he said exultantly. 'Uncle Philip's car is green! Right, are we off to beard him in his den?'

I hesitated.

'Come on,' Liam said. 'The police will be checking out all the family cars. We need to get in first!'

'But if Philip is dangerous . . .'

'Come on, Aunt Madge,' Liam pleaded. 'We'll be really careful. And subtle. You know you want to find out who killed Great Aunt Pepper!'

*   *   *

Philip's house was semi-detached—for the first time I realised how similar it was to George's. How similar their lives had been. The only real difference was that George had been married and divorced twice, Philip only once.

The drive was empty; Liam

bounded up to the front door and pressed the bell long and hard. We heard it chime inside.

'He's out!' Liam said indignantly.

Footsteps round the side of the house; Uncle Philip, in shirt sleeves and a pristine gardening apron, glared at us. 'This is an honour,' he said sarcastically.

Liam started forward. 'Where's your car?!'

So much for the subtle approach. I grabbed Liam, held him back. 'Was it you who ran cousin Martin down?'

Philip nodded, unabashed. 'After you were so pig-headed, I thought I'd try and talk him out of seeing you again. But then I saw him on the pavement and couldn't resist taking a swipe at him. It was all that talk about people knocking the Pepper into the ditch that gave me the idea.' He raised an eyebrow. 'No point in looking at me like that, you know. Just wanted to frighten him off. Hardly touched him. And, what's more, it was entirely *your* fault—if you hadn't made me so angry I'd never have done it.'

'*My* fault?' I said, furious. Liam was outraged; I hushed him. 'Since you're in the mood for confessions, Philip, I want to know what happened on the night Great Aunt Pepper died. I mean, what *really* happened.'

'I've already told you,' he said impatiently. 'The woman was wild with anger and didn't know what she was doing. She walked into a ditch in the dark and drowned.'

'Walked?' I said. 'Or was pushed?'

'And who pushed her?' Liam demanded.

Philip gave him a long considering look. 'What it is to be young,' he said with a note of false admiration. 'To be so convinced that if the truth is known, everything will be well.'

Liam flushed. I put a hand on his arm. 'I think the voice you're really hearing, Liam, is Great Aunt

Pepper's. You may have hated her, Philip, but I bet you sound just like she did. Sour and nasty.'

He bared his teeth in a snarl. 'Think you know it all, don't you? Oh, very well! If you *must* know! But not here. Follow me!'

He led us round the side of the house, into the back garden. It was immaculate: a smooth unblemished spread of lawn, flowerbeds bright with pink and yellow roses, mature trees sheltering the garden from prying eyes. The truth of what Philip had been doing was on a table on the decking: a half-empty whiskey bottle and a full glass, next to a folded *Times* that looked untouched.

Philip lowered himself into his seat, gestured for me to take the only other chair. Liam lounged against the wall of the house. Philip raised his glass in a toast. 'To your persistence, Margaret. You always were an annoying pest.'

Liam started to say something

indignant; I said, 'Tell us what happened, and we'll leave you in peace.'

He stared into his whisky glass. 'If you'd had to live in that household, you'd know how impossible that woman was. That's what happens to unmarried women—they end up looking after other people's kids and resenting every minute of it.' He cast a pointed glance at me, then at Liam; I had to hush Liam again.

'She was impossible to please,' Philip said. 'Whatever you did was wrong. Of course, we boys could always dash off somewhere—to play with friends, or to some club or other. Jane got the worst of it— the Pepper was always on at her to learn the proper way for a young lady to behave if she wanted to catch a husband. As if the Pepper knew!' He smiled at me. 'What is it with you spinsters?'

'Just get on with the story.'

He shrugged. 'Jane rebelled. She

had a date and you know what girls of sixteen are like when a young man takes an interest in them. She was all for going, even though the weather was dreadful.' He raised his eyes to heaven. 'You should have heard the screaming and shrieking! And of course in the end, Jane dashed out for the bus with the Pepper trailing along behind and forecasting everything from pneumonia to eternal damnation!'

He studied the whisky thoughtfully. 'There was a struggle, halfway to the bus-stop. The Pepper grabbed hold of Jane, she struggled to be free. She pushed the Pepper. And she went down into the ditch.' He chuckled. 'George and I were watching from the front door. We thought it a great lark. Jane ran off and caught the bus and we went back in and made ourselves scarce because we didn't want to be around when the Pepper squelched in, sodden to the skin. Three hours later, in the middle of a game of ping-pong, we suddenly realised she hadn't come back. By then, it was too late.'

He grimaced. 'Come on, Margaret. It was an accident! Jane didn't mean to kill the Pepper. What were we supposed to do? Throw her to the wolves?'

'The coroner might have decided it was accidental death.'

'Or he might have thrown Jane in jail! And for what? For ridding the world of a sour old woman who was making everyone's lives a misery?'

Liam choked suddenly, said vehemently, 'You're *horrid*,' and ran off round the side of the house.

I got up. 'I agree with Liam,' I said. 'But thank you for your candour. I daresay it will quite a while before we see each other again.'

I heard him laughing softly as I left.

At the front of the house, Liam was kicking the garden wall viciously.

'Now what?' he said, angrily. 'We tell Martin his stepmother was a murderess?'

Could we just pretend that Philip had never told us anything? But Martin already suspected Jane might have been involved in Great Aunt Pepper's death and he didn't seem the sort of man who would simply let the matter drop—particularly after the accident. 'I think we have to.'

*   *   *

Martin broke into a broad grin when he opened the door of his hotel room. 'I didn't expect to see you till tonight. Come on in. I got something to show you.'

Liam nudged me as we walked into the room, mouthed *Tell him*. Suddenly, I wasn't sure I could.

On a small table in one corner of the room, a laptop was open and glowing. 'Come see this,' Martin said and clicked on an icon. 'These are the pictures mom gave dad,' he said. 'Look.'

I had to do it now or I'd never summon up the courage. 'Martin,' I started—

On the laptop's screen, a slide show started to unroll. Old photographs, mainly black and white. Uncles George and Philip, in cricket whites, looking startlingly young— late teens, probably. My father, startled in the middle of reading a book, glancing up in some irritation. Aunt Jane, petulant and rebellious in a huge apron. And—

'Wait!' I caught Martin's arm. 'Can you go back to that last one? Pause it.'

'Sure.' The photograph popped back up. It wasn't very well taken— someone's head poked into the bottom left-hand corner of the frame. A young George was visible on the right, laughing uproariously. In the middle of the frame was a middle-aged Great Aunt Pepper in coat and ugly hat, holding off a very small figure. A young girl, with fists raised to batter at Great Aunt Pepper's chest. Great Aunt Pepper looked as amused as George but in a far more sinister fashion . . .

'Is that Aunt Jane?' Liam said in a strangled voice.

'No way,' Martin said. 'You can see Mom at the back—by the door. She looks about sixteen so it can't have been very long before the old lady died. I don't know who the child is.'

'I do,' I said.

*   *   *

Judith was sitting at the kitchen table, tapping into her laptop, when Tamsin slammed the door behind me. She looked up irritably, said, 'Not now, Madge. I've far too much work to do.'

I put the photograph down on the table, pushed it towards her.

'Remember this?'

Her gaze settled on it, stilled. There was a moment's silence.

'Philip told me earlier today that Aunt Jane killed Great Aunt Pepper.'

'Well,' she said brightly. 'He should know. He was there, after all.'

She got up with a fine display of nonchalance, poured coffee from the expensive percolator. She didn't offer me any. 'I hope this is important. I have to finish these spreadsheets before the end of the day.'

'It's important,' I said, sitting down opposite her. 'Murder always is.'

She put her mug down on the table with a loud click. 'Get to the point, Madge.'

'The point is,' I said, 'that Aunt Jane is safely dead and her only close living relative—apart from us—is a stepson who didn't get on with her. Philip calculated he could safely accuse her of murder without hurting

85

anyone's feelings. Which argues—' I overrode her as she started to speak, 'that Philip was protecting someone. And you know—I've always thought of Philip as supremely selfish. So who might he want to protect?' I tapped the photo. 'How about a seven year old child who didn't really understand what she was doing?'

Judith said nothing.

'It was while I was ill, wasn't it?' I said. 'While you were staying with grandfather.'

'That horrible woman,' Judith said. 'She was a bully and a killjoy.'

I thought of the smile on Great Aunt Pepper's face as she held off the seven-year-old Judith. 'She still didn't deserve to die.'

'You didn't know her,' she said. 'You didn't see the way she looked at me, and told me I wasn't any good, and no one loved me, and mum and dad always put you first, because otherwise they wouldn't have sent me away.'

'They didn't want you to catch measles too!'

Judith laughed bitterly. 'Good old Madge, always twisting things to suit yourself.'

'I do not!' I started angrily, then stopped. Arguing with Judith was not going to help get at the truth.

'I should have known something like this would happen,' she said contemptuously. 'As soon as you retired, and weren't wanted any more.'

Something squeezed at my heart.

'Of course they gave you a fine send-off at work,' she said, 'but have you heard from any of them since?'

'It's been less than a week.'

'Don't get your hopes up,' she said. 'Well, I've had my revenge on you, Madge. Two marriages for me, and a son at the first attempt, and a first-class, highly-paid prestigious job into the bargain. No more cast-off clothes, no more having to listen to how well you did in exams, or how pretty you looked.'

I said nothing. I knew what she was referring to—I'd been embarrassed as a child, even as I basked in the praise. What Judith didn't know about, of course, were the times Mum and Dad had held *her* up to *me* as a shining example of good manners and behaviour. And I kept quiet too because I suddenly realised what Great Aunt Pepper must have felt like: how galling it must have been to have to look after five children who must always have been comparing her unfavourably with their mother.

'So what happened?' I asked.

She shrugged, almost indifferently. 'I tried to run away but she caught me. It was wet. She was yelling at me. Saying horrible things, like how bad I was, and how no one wanted me. So I pushed her. She was standing just in front of the ditch and she fell in, with a great splash and a shriek.'

'And then?'

She shrugged. 'I can't remember.' She looked at the photograph, pushed it back towards me. 'I don't regret it, you know. I *wanted* to hurt her.'

Of course she had—under the circumstances, I would have felt exactly the same. And possibly done the same thing. A push, a satisfying shriek and a splash. A seven-year-old wouldn't understand how badly it all might go wrong. But teenagers would: Philip and Jane and George would have known exactly the dangers and they hadn't raised a finger to help Great Aunt Pepper. I'd been right—Philip was much too selfish to protect anyone but himself.

Judith got up to pour more coffee. 'If you don't mind, Madge—I have work to do . . .'

I left her musing over the laptop and went back down the corridor towards the front door with Great Aunt Pepper's picture in my hand. However much I pitied her—and she certainly hadn't deserved to die like that—Aunt Pepper had a lot to answer for. She was the one who'd made George, Philip and Judith the people they were today: insecure, combative, always defending their own positions by putting other people down. And it was far too late to do anything to help any of them. At least Liam had been strong-willed enough to resist copying his mother.

The living room door opened; Tamsin hesitated on the threshold. The music, thankfully, was off. Behind her, on the settee, was a mobile phone, glittering brightly—and an old stuffed teddy bear, threadbare and tattered. Much-loved, obviously.

Too late to do anything?

'I'm thinking of adopting a cat,' I said on impulse. 'I was going to the rescue place tomorrow to choose one. Want to come?'

She hesitated, looked at me for a long time. Then she turned up her nose and sneered.

'Oh well,' I said, 'Let me know if you change your mind.'

She didn't respond. I went to the door, let myself out into the street.

On the doorstep, I paused for a moment, the photograph in my hand. Behind me, Judith called out sharply. A moment's silence, then the music blared out.

Did I wish I'd never started researching my family history? In a way. Living in the past has its own dangers. Hadn't Judith's life always been a reaction against what she thought of as the unfairness of her upbringing—resentments nurtured and cherished by Great Aunt Pepper? As for me—

Was I going to spend the next few years wondering what was going on at work and hoping they'd contact me?

I put the photo in my bag, hunted in my pockets for my mobile, rang the Cavendish Hotel. When I got through to Martin's room, his voice was formal until he realised who I was. 'Madge! Hey!'

'You know that arrangement we have for dinner?' I said.

His voice dulled. 'You can't make it?'

'I was wondering,' I said, 'if you'd care to have tea as well.'

'English tea and scones?' he asked.

'With cream and strawberry jam.'

'Can't wait,' he said.

Neither could I.